Great Start!

**Purchased with
Smart Start Funds**

Down the Winding Road

story by Angela Johnson ❦ illustrations by Shane W. Evans

DORLING KINDERSLEY PUBLISHING, INC.

To Mattie Floyd with love
—A. J.

I would like to thank GOD, and dedicate this book
to my grandmother and grandfather
(my Old Ones) for playing a major role
in who I am today.
—S. W. E.

A Richard Jackson Book

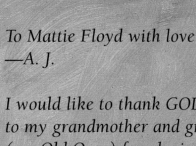

Dorling Kindersley Publishing, Inc., 95 Madison Avenue, New York, New York 10016
Visit us on the World Wide Web at http://www.dk.com

Library of Congress Cataloging-in-Publication Data
Johnson, Angela.
Down the winding road / story by Angela Johnson;
illustrations by Shane Evans.—1st ed.
p.   cm.
"A Richard Jackson book"—T.p. verso.
Summary: The annual summer visit to the country
home of the Old Ones, the uncles and aunts who
raised Daddy, brings joy and good times.
ISBN 0-7894-2596-3
[1. Country life—Fiction. 2. Family life—Fiction.
3. Afro-Americans—Fiction.]   I. Evans, Shane, ill.
II. Title.
PZ7.J629 Dq 2000   [E]—dc21   99-041102

Book design by Jennifer Browne.
The illustrations for this book were painted using oils.
The text of this book is set in 21 point Berkeley.
Printed and bound in U.S.A.

First Edition, 2000
10 9 8 7 6 5 4 3 2 1

We take the winding road every year.
Past the city,
way past all the people
to the Old Ones' house.

They are Daddy's uncles and aunts,
who raised him and live down the winding road
and are standing in line when we
pull into the drive.

Two
four
six
seven of them. . .

All in a row,
looking just alike.

Hugging just alike
with creased faces
and warm hands to hold.

Daddy's people have been the
Old Ones since he could remember,
and since I can remember, too.

Then the Old Ones take me and my brother Jesse
on a long walk
through the grassy woods
that stretch along the winding road.

They show us the trees that they climbed
and tell us stories about them
that they all know by heart. . . .

". . . and remember the time, May, you got stuck
up in the maple all night long,
with us calling you until the sun came up?"

"... and the way you ate up everybody's breakfast
the next morning and got so sick
Mama had to stay with you all day long?"

"... and wasn't it sad when they cut down
the old-growth trees around here
to put up more highway?"

Then Jesse and me and the Old Ones
walk to the lake that they swam in
when they were young—
and sit beside now that they are old.

Beneath the hanging willow Jesse finds
an old tire swing
and before we know it,
we're flying high
over the lake.

And the Old Ones stand at the shore
clapping, laughing, and yelling.

"Higher!" They shout.
"Isn't it wonderful?" They laugh.
And then. . .
"There's nothing like flying!"

And there is nothing like flying
as me and Jesse let go of the swing
and fly into the lake in our clothes. . . .

The lake glimmers beside the winding road.
Jesse and I chase each other in the water,
then watch the trees and the Old Ones
to know when it's time to go.

The Old Ones talk about this time,
and that time,
and they sure had a good time. . . .

Then we walk again along
the winding road for home,
slowing down a bit for the Old Ones.

It's our last day of summer vacation
and we have spent it with the Old Ones,
but now it's time to go.

As we get in our car
they line up in a row;
looking just alike, with creased faces.

Then they wave us away,

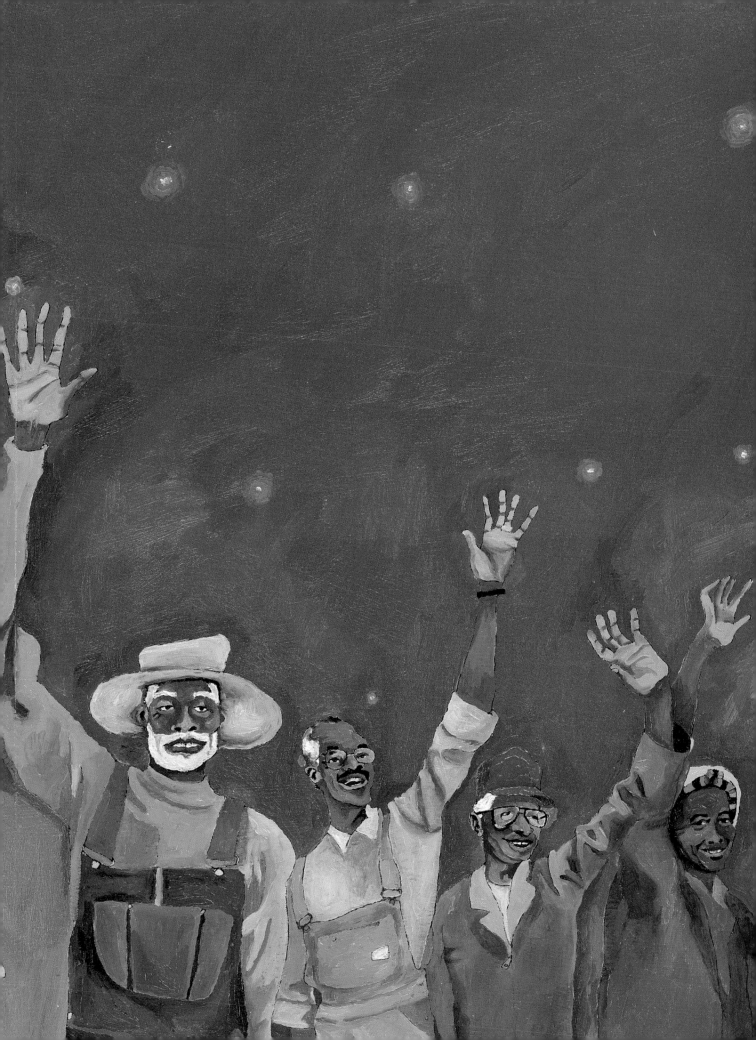

back to the city,
and we are already missing them

along the winding road.